When Ozzy Ocelot Forgot

Level 10 – White

King's Lynn, Norfolk PE30 4LS

ISBN 978-1-83927-017-8

 Printed in Malaysia.
A catalogue record for this book is available from the British Library.

When Ozzy Ocelot Forgot
Written by Shalini Vallepur
Illustrated by Rosie Groom

An Introduction to BookLife Readers...

Our Readers have been specifically created in line with the London Institute of Education's approach to book banding and are phonetically decodable and ordered to support each phase of the Letters and Sounds document.

Each book has been created to provide the best possible reading and learning experience. Our aim is to share our love of books with children, providing both emerging readers and prolific page-turners with beautiful books that are guaranteed to provoke interest and learning, regardless of ability.

BOOK BAND GRADED using the Institute of Education's approach to levelling.

PHONETICALLY DECODABLE supporting each phase of Letters and Sounds.

EXERCISES AND QUESTIONS to offer reinforcement and to ascertain comprehension.

BEAUTIFULLY ILLUSTRATED to inspire and provoke engagement, providing a variety of styles for the reader to enjoy whilst reading through the series.

AUTHOR INSIGHT:
SHALINI VALLEPUR

Passionate about books from a very young age, Shalini Vallepur received the award of Norfolk County Scholar for her outstanding grades. Later on she read English at the University of Leicester, where she stayed to complete her Modern Literature MA. Whilst at university, Shalini volunteered as a storyteller to help children learn to read, which gave her experience and expertise in the way children pick up and retain information. She used her knowledge and her background and implemented them in the 32 books that she has written for BookLife Publishing. Shalini's writing easily takes us to different worlds, and the serenity and quality of her words are sure to captivate any child who picks up her books.

This book focuses on developing independence, fluency and comprehension. It is a white level 10 book band.

When Ozzy Ocelot Forgot

Written by
Shalini Vallepur

Illustrated by
Rosie Groom

Chapter One

Me and My Friends

My name is Ozzy Ocelot, and I love life in the Amazon rainforest. I'm a little forgetful, but it doesn't matter, because my only job is to have fun with my friends. I love my friends. Let me tell you about them...

There's Connor Crocodile. He can be a little snappy, but he's quite nice most of the time. Polina Parrot is one of my oldest friends. She's chatty, cheerful and enjoys a good gossip. Solomon Sloth is oh so slow, but he's super friendly.
Frank Frog is the sort of friend you go to when you want to laugh your socks off.

Lastly, there's Fancy Flamingo. She's a top-notch friend. Fancy Flamingo deserves a gold medal. She's bold, clever and strong, and she's got the prettiest pink feathers.

Fancy Flamingo is everyone's best friend.

But something happened last week. I did something awful. I forgot something very important. I forgot that it was Fancy Flamingo's birthday!

I'll tell you all about what happened and how I managed to fix it.

Chapter Two

The Invitation

It all started when I had hot chocolate with Polina.

"I'm so excited for tonight! I've got everything ready," Polina giggled.

"Why? What's going on?" I asked, as I sipped on my hot chocolate.

"Ozzy! It's Fancy Flamingo's birthday party tonight. You didn't forget, did you?" said Polina.
"Oh golly, I think I forgot!" I said. "She never gave me an invitation!"
"You're so forgetful, Ozzy! Everybody got an invitation! Don't you remember? I'll show you," said Polina.

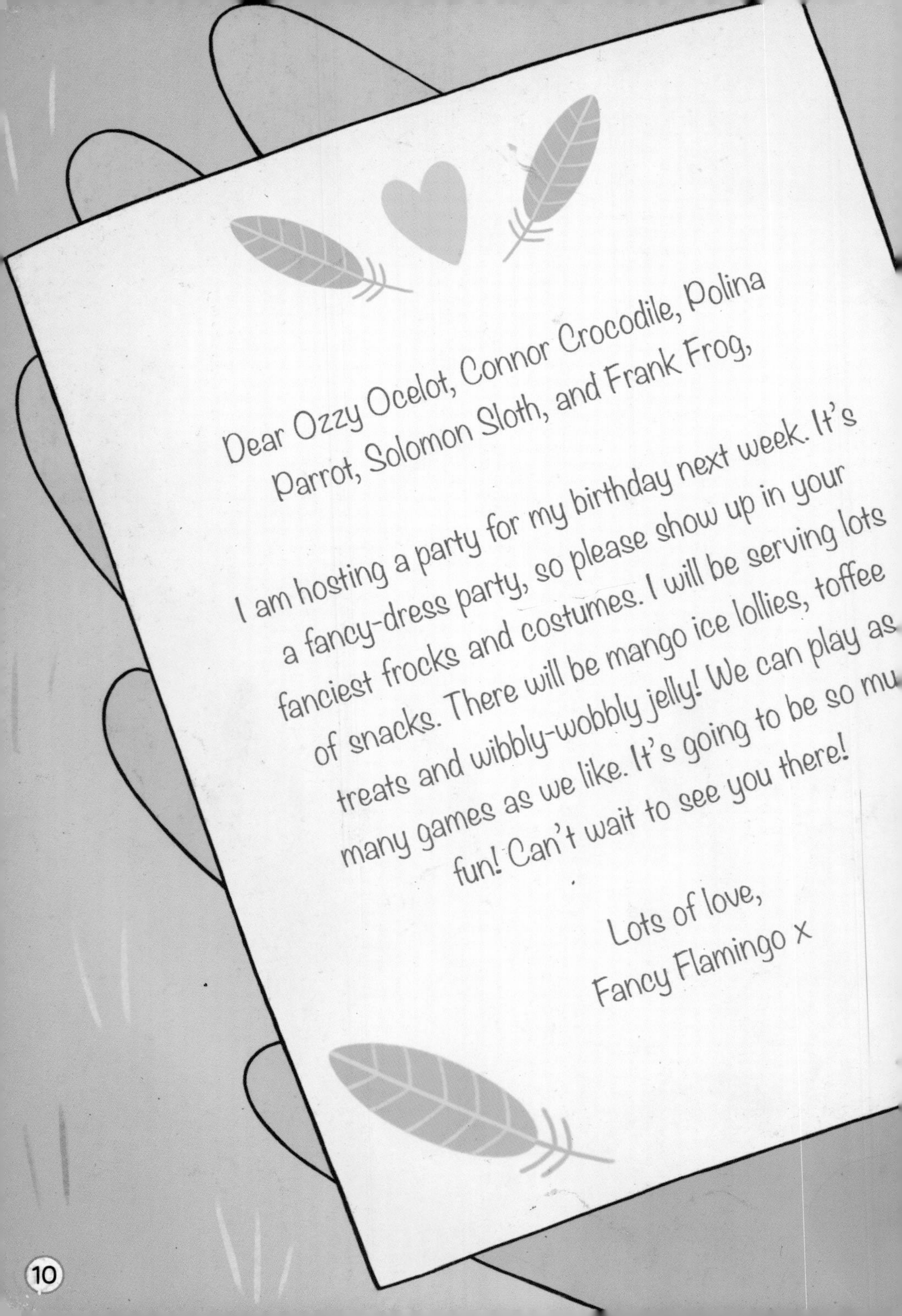

Dear Ozzy Ocelot, Connor Crocodile, Polina Parrot, Solomon Sloth, and Frank Frog,

I am hosting a party for my birthday next week. It's a fancy-dress party, so please show up in your fanciest frocks and costumes. I will be serving lots of snacks. There will be mango ice lollies, toffee treats and wibbly-wobbly jelly! We can play as many games as we like. It's going to be so mu fun! Can't wait to see you there!

Lots of love,
Fancy Flamingo x

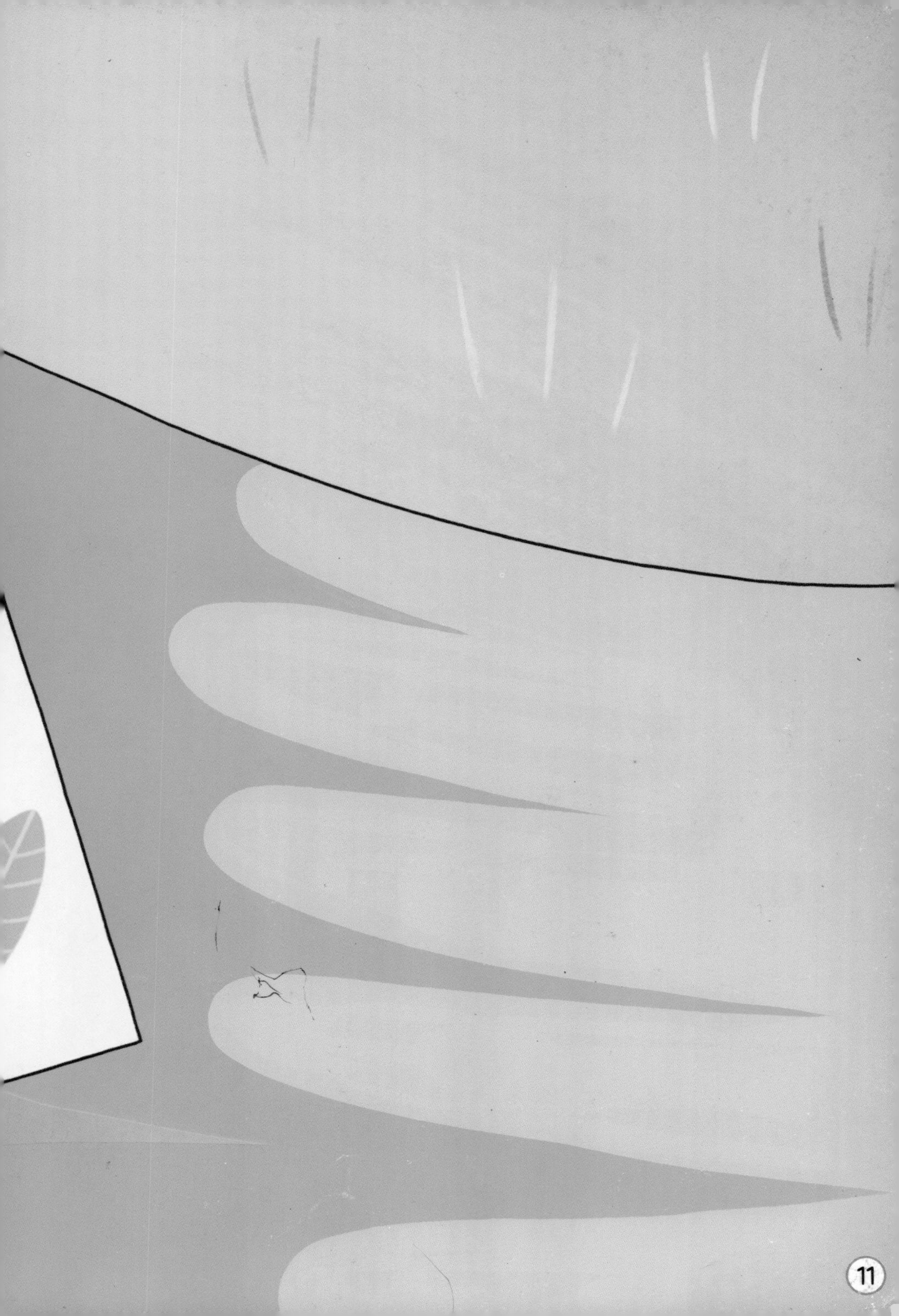

Chapter Three

All Over the Amazon

"Oh no, what should I do? I'm so forgetful!" I said. I couldn't believe that I had forgotten about my best friend's birthday.

"You've got the rest of the day to find a present. Go out there and get something!" said Polina.

"I got Fancy a lovely bonnet. It's blue and has peacock feathers all over it."

"Ok, I won't get Fancy a peacock bonnet. Thanks for reminding me, Polina," I said. I gulped down the rest of my hot chocolate and dashed away. The party was later on that day, so I didn't have a lot of time.

I ran straight to the swamp. It was foggy and cold, and nobody was around. I looked for a possible present. As I got closer to the swamp, I noticed something lurking in the water.

It got closer, and closer, until...
SPLASH! Connor Crocodile appeared.
"Hello, Ozzy. What brings you to my swamp?" asked Connor.
"I'm looking for a present for Fancy," I said.
"The party is today, Ozzy! Let me guess... You forgot to get her something?" said Connor.

"Yes, I forgot. What present did you get for Fancy?" I asked.
"I got Fancy a pair of golden goggles. I wear some whenever I go pond dipping. Now Fancy can do the same when she goes dipping," said Connor.
"She's always wanted a pair of golden goggles! I wish that I hadn't forgotten," I said.
"Well, that's your fault," Connor snapped. "You better head back into the rainforest and look for something there."

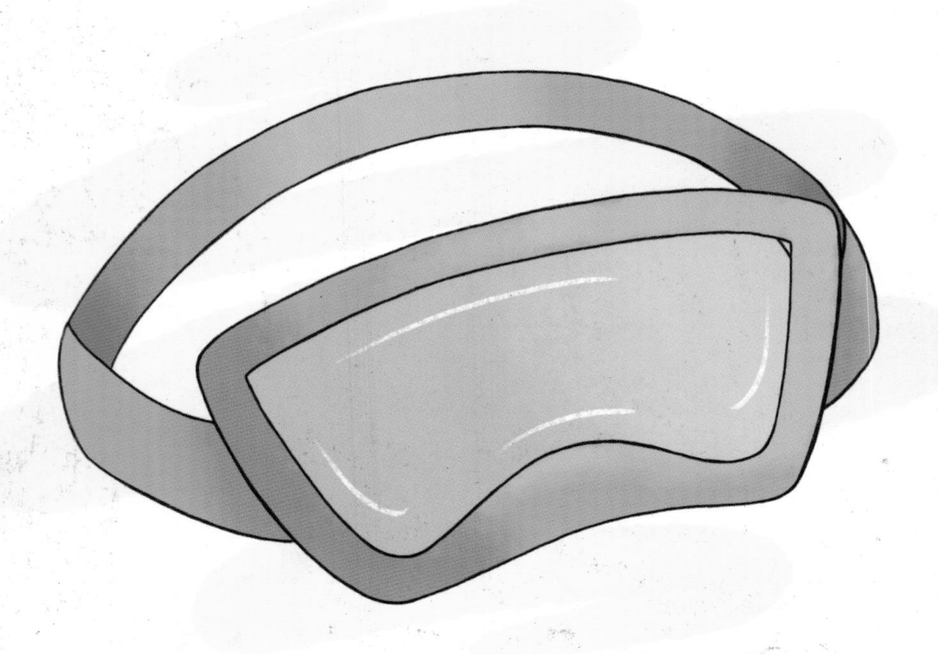

I went back into the rainforest to look for a present. Both Solomon Sloth and Frank Frog were hanging out in the trees.
"Yoo-hoo! Ozzy! Up here!" Frank called from high up in the trees.
"Solomon! Frank! I forgot to get Fancy a birthday present. I need some help!" I shouted.

"Well, I got Fancy this old potato. Isn't it neat?" said Solomon. He held up a potato that was small and spotty.
"It's a bit gross, Solomon. I'm not sure Fancy will like it," I said. I was just being honest.

"Nonsense! Fancy loves potatoes!" said Solomon Sloth with a grin.

"At least Solomon got a present for Fancy! You forgot!" said Frank. He pulled out a toy rocket. "I got this cool toy rocket for Fancy. She'll be flying through the skies in no time!"

Chapter Four

The Cake Mistake and Bursting Balloons

I left Solomon and Frank and sat on a rock by myself. I couldn't find a good present and nobody would help me. I didn't know what to get Fancy. I thought about the things that Fancy had got me before. She once baked a cake for my birthday.

That was it! I decided to bake a cake for Fancy.

I got all the ingredients ready to bake a cake. It was going to be a toffee cake. I looked at the ingredient list once, twice and then again for a third time. I wasn't going to forget anything this time! I took a big bowl and got to work. I poured the cake batter from the big bowl into a tin and then popped it into the oven. It was going to take an hour to bake, so I curled up on the sofa and dozed off.

I woke up to the smell of burning. Yikes! I forgot to set a timer! I totally forgot about the cake! I dashed to the oven, turned it off and looked inside. The cake was black and ruined. Nobody could eat it and I didn't have time to try and fix it.

So, the cake went wrong, but I still wanted to bring something to the party. I had a brilliant idea to bring some balloons – everyone loves balloons, right?

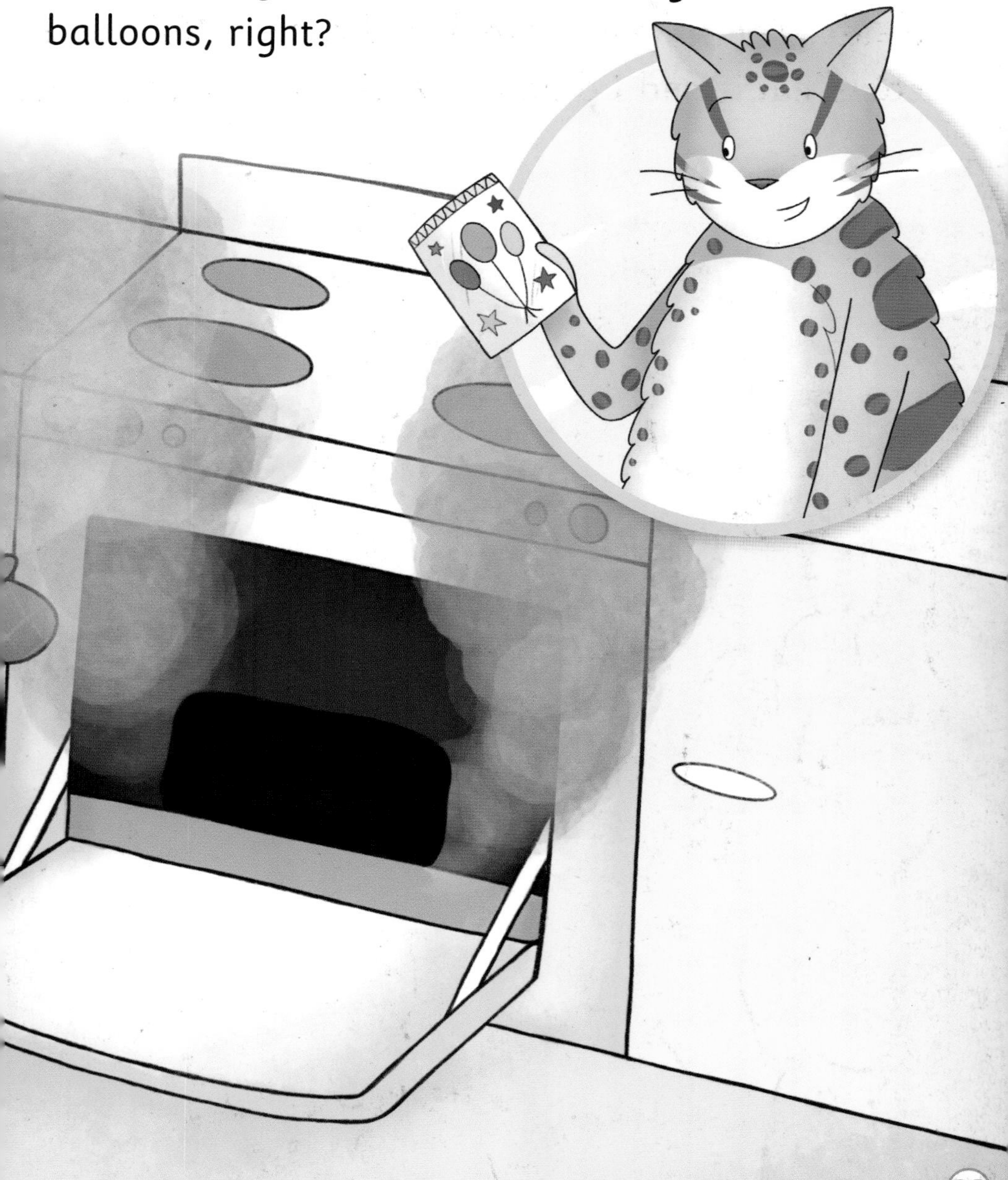

I blew and blew and blew. It was going well. I was so happy that I had finally found something to bring to the party. The balloon got bigger and bigger and bigger until... POP! It burst in my face!

I looked down at my paws and saw my long claws sticking out. Darn! I forgot that I had claws and my claws had popped the balloon! I was back to square one.

Chapter Five

The Sock

I was almost out of time. The party was going to start! I ran around the rainforest looking for a present for Fancy. I was zooming past the rocks by the river when I saw a bright pink object. It was a long sock.
It was almost time for the party and I didn't have time to look for anything else. I grabbed the sock and made my way to Fancy's house for the party.

Chapter Six

The Party

I arrived at the party and looked around. Oh dear. I was so busy looking for a present that I forgot it was a fancy-dress party! Everybody was dressed up in fancy frocks and silly costumes. They looked amazing.

Connor was a cowboy. He was wearing a floppy cowboy hat and boots on his four feet. Solomon looked great. He had come as a ladybird. He had painted his fur red and he had black blobs all over his body.

Polina was covered in a white sheet. She had come as a spooky ghost! She was flying above everybody, making spooky noises.

Frank had come as a prince. He was wearing a little gold crown on top of his head.

Fancy was dressed as a ballerina. She had a big tutu on but I could see that she was missing one of her socks. I felt like a silly mango without a costume. I wanted to leave but Fancy spotted me and came over.

"Oh, Ozzy, you forgot to wear a costume," said Fancy. "Don't worry. If you have a present, then please put it on the tabletop."

"I'm so sorry, Fancy. I forgot to get a costume," I said. "I also forgot to wrap your present, so here it is." I gave Fancy the long pink sock. Fancy's face lit up.

"You found my sock, Ozzy!" said Fancy with a smile. "It fell out of my pocket when I was walking through the rainforest. I thought it was lost forever!"

"I'm so glad I found it. Happy birthday, Fancy Flamingo!" I said.
"Thank you so much! Now I don't have to walk around wearing one sock!" laughed Fancy.

"Come on, Ozzy, let's go and enjoy the party!" I spent the rest of the day with my friends in the rainforest, and I didn't forget to have fun!

When Ozzy Ocelot Forgot

1. Who did Ozzy have a hot chocolate with?

2. What was the swamp like?

3. Where was Frank Frog hanging out?

4. What did Solomon Sloth get Fancy Flamingo?

   (a) A blue hat

   (b) An old potato

   (c) A red balloon

5. How do you think Ozzy felt when he turned up to the party without a costume? Have you ever felt like this?

Helpful Hints for Reading at Home

The focus phonemes (units of sound) used throughout this series are in line with the order in which your child is taught at school. This offers a consistent approach to learning whether reading at home or in the classroom.

HERE ARE SOME COMMON WORDS THAT YOUR CHILD MIGHT FIND TRICKY:

water	where	would	know	thought	through	couldn't
laughed	eyes	once	we're	school	can't	our

TOP TIPS FOR HELPING YOUR CHILD TO READ:

- Encourage your child to read aloud as well as silently to themselves.
- Allow your child time to absorb the text and make comments.
- Ask simple questions about the text to assess understanding.
- Encourage your child to clarify the meaning of new vocabulary.

This book focuses on developing independence, fluency and comprehension. It is a white level 10 book band.